LOVED

TO BITS

Teresa Heapy & Katie Cleminson

David Fickling Books

My ted's special.
Stripy Ted.

He's not allowed
to leave my bed.

For long ago, he was . . .

. . . a super, somersaulting ted,

all golden stripes
from foot to head,

who made adventures
round my bed
from dreams we had,
and books we read.

We foiled the plot,

we fought the beast,

we rode,

we hid, we found the feast.

We tickled
monsters,

fled on rafts,

we searched,

explored,

escaped . . .

and laughed.

And if I stumbled,
back he sped
to rescue me,
with arms outspread.

"Take my paw . . .

and
ONWARDS!"

said my furry,
funny, fearless ted.

There was the time
he tumbled

SPLOSH!

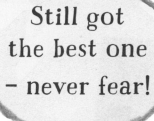
Splendid
stuff!
I love a wash!

There was the
time he lost
an ear –

Still got
the best one
– never fear!

And then the time his eye went

PING!

"It's nothing! Didn't feel a thing!"

And once, within a tug-of-war . . .

And once, his leg got tangled,

. . . thump!

he slipped.

I caught
his paw.

I held him
tightly

just

once

more.

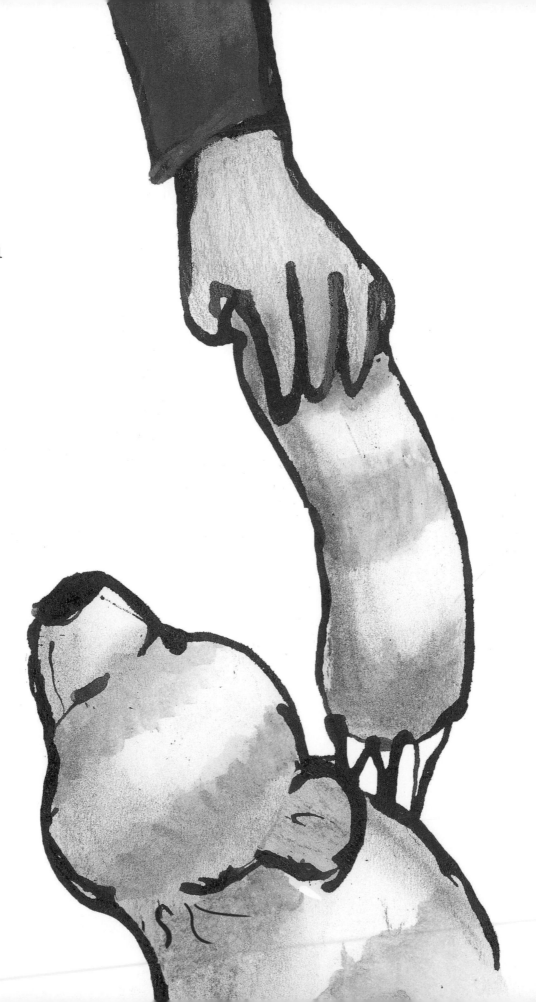

But

in the end . . .

the

last

stitch

tore

and

Stripy Ted

fell

to

the

floor.

I picked him up.

A scruffy ted.

No arms and legs –
just hanging threads.

Stripes loved off,
all brown instead.

Battered,

worn-out

ball and head.

Mum reached for him.

"Poor little ted.
Shall I mend him?"

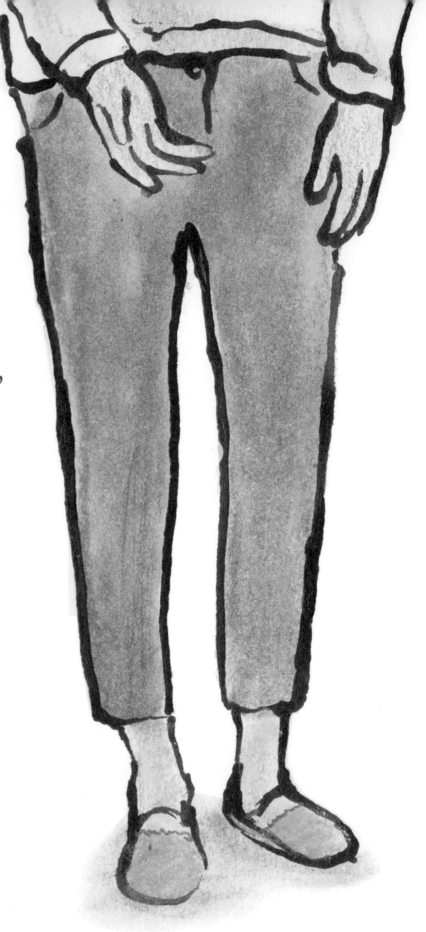

"No," I said.

The truth

was now,

I liked him better.

I could hold him in one hand.

He fitted right,

just here.

He knows my hopes,
my secret schemes,

my stories,
wishes,
fears and
dreams.

Yes, my ted's special.
Stripy Ted.

And he belongs with me in bed.